and the
Circus Mystery

A Viking Easy-to-Read

BY **D**AVID **A.** **A**DLER

ILLUSTRATED BY **S**USANNA **N**ATTI

VIKING
An Imprint of Penguin Group (USA) Inc.

For my friends
Sara Rose, JaJa, Danielle, Sam, Maayan, and Ben
—D.A.

For Hannah Rose and Mason
—S.N.

VIKING
Published by Penguin Group
Penguin Young Readers Group, 345 Hudson Street, New York, New York 10014, U.S.A.
Penguin Group (Canada), 90 Eglinton Avenue East, Suite 700, Toronto, Ontario, Canada M4P 2Y3
(a division of Pearson Penguin Canada Inc.)
Penguin Books Ltd, 80 Strand, London WC2R 0RL, England
Penguin Ireland, 25 St Stephen's Green, Dublin 2, Ireland (a division of Penguin Books Ltd)
Penguin Group (Australia), 250 Camberwell Road, Camberwell, Victoria 3124, Australia
(a division of Pearson Australia Group Pty Ltd)
Penguin Books India Pvt Ltd, 11 Community Centre, Panchsheel Park, New Delhi – 110 017, India
Penguin Group (NZ), 67 Apollo Drive, Rosedale, North Shore 0632, New Zealand
(a division of Pearson New Zealand Ltd)
Penguin Books (South Africa) (Pty) Ltd, 24 Sturdee Avenue, Rosebank, Johannesburg 2196, South Africa

Penguin Books Ltd, Registered Offices: 80 Strand, London WC2R 0RL, England

First published in 2011 by Viking, a division of Penguin Young Readers Group

3 5 7 9 10 8 6 4 2

LIBRARY OF CONGRESS CATALOGING-IN-PUBLICATION DATA
Adler, David A.
Young Cam Jansen and the circus mystery / David A. Adler ; illustrated
by Susanna Natti.
p. cm. — (Young Cam Jansen ; 17)
ISBN 978-0-670-01242-8 (hardcover)
[1. Circus—Fiction. 2. Lost and found possessions—Fiction. 3. Mystery
and detective stories.] I. Natti, Susanna, ill. II. Title.
PZ7.A2615Caaec 2011
[E]—dc22
2010031961

Manufactured in China
Set in Bookman

CONTENTS

1. I Could Be a Clown 4

2. Oops! Did I Step on Your Foot? 9

3. I Think I Know What Happened 18

4. *BAM!* 22

5. Another Parade 26

A Cam Jansen Memory Game 32

1. I Could Be a Clown

"Look at me,"

Cam Jansen's aunt Molly said.

Aunt Molly stuck out her tongue.

She put her hands behind her head

and waved them.

"Aren't I funny? I could be a clown."

Cam, her friend Eric Shelton,

and Aunt Molly were in line

to buy tickets to the circus.

"I want to sit in the first row,"

Aunt Molly said.

"I want to make the clowns laugh."

"I want to sit high up," Eric said.

"I want to get a good look

at the tightrope walker."

Cam closed her eyes.

She said, *"Click!"*

With her eyes still closed she said,

"We can sit in the first row for the parade.

All the clowns will be in the parade.

Then we can sit high up.

This circus lets us change seats."

"How do you know that?"

an old man in line asked.

Cam said, "I'm looking at a circus poster.

It says, 'Open seating.'"

"But your eyes are closed," the old man said.

"Cam has an amazing memory," Eric told him.

"She has a picture in her head

of the circus poster.

She has pictures in her head

of everything she's seen."

"What else is on the poster?"

the old man asked.

"In the middle is a clown," Cam said.

"At the bottom of the poster

are elephants, tigers, giraffes, and monkeys."

Cam opened her eyes.

The old man said,

"You really do have an amazing memory."

"When I want to remember something,"

Cam told him, "I just close my eyes

and say, *'Click!'*"

Cam pointed to her head.

"That's the sound the camera up here makes."

Eric told the man, "Her real name is Jennifer,

but because of her great memory

we started calling her 'The Camera.'

Then 'The Camera' became just 'Cam.'"

"I have the tickets," Aunt Molly said.

"Let's go inside."

2. Oops! Did I Step on Your Foot?

Aunt Molly, Cam, and Eric entered a large hall.

"Programs! Programs!" a woman called out.

"Get your circus programs here!"

"Caramel popcorn!" someone else shouted.

"Peanuts! Cotton candy! Soda!

Ice-cold water!"

Aunt Molly bought an extra-large box

of caramel popcorn.

She showed her tickets to a woman

standing by a large open door.

Then Aunt Molly, Cam, and Eric

walked into the circus arena.

In the center of the arena was a large ring.

Around the ring were rows and rows of seats.

"Let's sit in front," Aunt Molly said.

"The parade is about to begin."

The clowns led the parade.

Aunt Molly put the popcorn box on her head.

She wrapped her scarf around the box.

She tied the scarf under her chin.

"Hey, look at me!" she called to the clowns.

"Look at my popcorn hat!"

A clown with a toy duck on his head stopped.

He laughed and pointed to the duck on his head.

"Quack! Quack!" the clown said.

Aunt Molly pointed to her popcorn hat

and said, "Pop! Pop!"

When the parade ended,

a short man wearing a big top hat came out.

"Welcome, welcome, welcome," he called out.

"The show is about to begin."

"Let's sit higher," Eric said.

He hurried up the stairs.

Aunt Molly took the popcorn box off her head.

Then she and Cam followed Eric.

Eric stopped near the top of the arena.

"Let's sit here," Eric called out.

"Excuse me," Aunt Molly said

to a large man with a small beard

at the end of the row.

"Oops!" she said as she squeezed past.

"Did I step on your foot?"

"Yes," the man said.

"I'm sorry," said Aunt Molly.

Cam and Eric walked very carefully

past the man and his small son.

"Let them by," a girl sitting next to the boy

told her mother.

"Look!" Eric called out, and pointed.

"Here come the dancing elephants."

The girl stood on her chair.

"Yeah!" she shouted.

She waved her cotton candy.

The cotton candy stuck to the boy's hair.

"Oops! I'm sorry," the girl said.

Cam and Eric ate some caramel popcorn.

Then Aunt Molly closed the box

and put it under her seat.

A clown sped around the ring

on a tiny tricycle.

He was chased by a clown in a police uniform.

Trill! Trill! The police clown blew a whistle.

"Look at that clown go!"

the girl shouted, and pointed.

When she pointed,

she knocked over the cup in her mother's hand.

Soda spilled on the boy.

"I'm so sorry," the woman said.

The man wiped the soda off his son's shirt.

Eric saw the spilled soda and said, "I'm thirsty."

"Let's get something to drink," Aunt Molly said.

"Please, excuse me," she said

to the girl and her mother.

"Please, excuse me," she said

to the man and his son.

"Excuse me. Excuse me," Cam and Eric said.

Aunt Molly, Cam, and Eric hurried

down the stairs.

They went to the hall just outside the

circus arena.

Aunt Molly bought three bottles of water.

Eric drank some water.

Then he said, "I'm going back."

Aunt Molly and Cam slowly followed him.

Cam looked up. "There's Eric," she said.

Aunt Molly and Cam walked up the stairs.

16

"Excuse me," they said to the large man

with the small beard and his son

at the end of the row.

"Here come the jugglers," Eric said.

Two women dressed as bakers came out.

They juggled large loaves of bread.

Eric looked at the bread and said, "Now I'm

hungry. I want some caramel popcorn."

Eric looked on the floor next to his seat.

He looked next to Aunt Molly's seat

and Cam's.

"Hey," Eric said. "Where's our popcorn?"

3. I Think I Know What Happened

"I left it under my seat," Aunt Molly said.

She looked under her seat.

She looked under Cam's and Eric's seats, too.

"The popcorn is gone," Aunt Molly said.

The short man with the top hat came out.

"Look to the high wire," he called out,

"for a great act of bravery and balance."

A tall, thin man in a blue cape

walked to the center of the ring.

He took off his cape and bowed.

Then he climbed a ladder to a small platform.

One end of a long wire

was attached to the platform.

The other end of the wire was attached

to another small platform

at the other end of the ring.

The man touched the wire with his foot.

The wire shook.

He pulled his foot back.

"Ooh!" people in the arena shouted.

Then they were quiet.

The man carefully stepped onto the wire.

He stretched his arms out to his sides

and slowly walked across the wire.

"This is scary," Aunt Molly said.

"I'm still hungry," Eric whispered.

"Sh," Aunt Molly told him.

Eric watched the tightrope walker

slowly walk to the other platform.

People in the arena cheered.

Eric looked at the man sitting

at the end of the row.

"Cam," Eric whispered.

"I think I know what happened

to our popcorn. I need you to look

at the picture in your head of that man."

Eric pointed to the large man with the

small beard at the end of the row.

"Did that man have a box of popcorn

when we went to get drinks?"

4. BAM!

Cam closed her eyes and said, *"Click!"*

"Yes," Cam said with her eyes closed.

"He did have popcorn."

"Look! Look!" Aunt Molly said.

"Here comes the cannon."

Clowns pushed a large cannon

to one side of the ring.

Clowns jumped and pointed at the cannon.

At its base was a long fuse.

Eric looked again at the popcorn box

at the end of his row.

"I bet I know what he did,"

Eric whispered to Cam.

"He finished his popcorn and was still hungry.

He took Aunt Molly's popcorn box

and put it in his empty box."

Two clowns brought out a ladder.

They set it by the mouth of the cannon.

The short man with the top hat came out.

"We end the show with a blast,"

he called out.

"Bullet Bob, the human cannonball,

will be shot into the air.

"Maybe he'll land near you."

A man wearing a silver cape

and a silver helmet came out.

He bowed, and people cheered.

Bullet Bob took off his silver cape.

He climbed into the mouth of the cannon.

Eric whispered to Cam,

"We have to get Aunt Molly's popcorn

before that man eats it all."

Bullet Bob waved.

He slid down the mouth of the cannon.

A clown lit the cannon's fuse.

Eric started walking toward

the man at the end of the row.

BAM!

Smoke filled the arena.

Small bits of silver paper

flew over Cam's head

to the highest parts of the arena.

Cam turned, but she didn't see Bullet Bob.

She saw something else.

"Wait!" Cam called to Eric. "Come back!"

5. Another Parade

Eric pointed to the box of caramel popcorn.

Cam shook her head.

Eric walked slowly back.

"There he is! There he is!"

a girl a few rows back shouted.

"There's Bullet Bob."

Clowns danced around a huge bed

at the other side of the ring.

In the middle of the bed was Bullet Bob.

"But that's our popcorn," Eric said.

"No, it's not," Cam told him.

"Our popcorn is three rows back."

Eric turned. Under a seat three rows back

was a large closed box of caramel popcorn.

"How did it get there?" Eric asked.

"It was always there," Cam said.

"Look at the noisy girl sitting in that row.

She's the girl we were sitting next to

at the beginning of the circus."

Eric looked at the girl.

Then he looked at the man and his son

at the end of their row.

"But he was sitting in our row, too," Eric said.

"When I saw him sitting here,

I was sure this was our row."

"He must have changed his seat," Cam said.

"Well, I'm still hungry," Eric said.

"I'm getting the popcorn."

"Excuse me," he said as he walked past

the man and his son.

Then Cam asked the man,

"Did you change your seats?"

"Yes," he said. "That girl

kept screaming and jumping.

She got cotton candy in my son's hair.

She spilled soda on him.

So we moved down a few rows."

Clowns marched into the center of the ring,

followed by dancing elephants.

"It's another parade," Aunt Molly said.

Aunt Molly opened her purse.

She took out a tube of red lipstick.

She painted red circles, squares,

and triangles on her face.

She puffed out her cheeks

and looked at the man at the end of the row.

The man laughed.

His son laughed.

"Let's go," Aunt Molly said.

"This time I'll make lots of clowns laugh."

Aunt Molly and Cam started down the steps.

"Wait for me," Eric called.

He was eating caramel popcorn

as he hurried toward Aunt Molly and Cam.

When Aunt Molly got to the edge of the ring

she waved at a clown.

The clown looked at Aunt Molly.

Aunt Molly puffed out her cheeks,

and the clown laughed.

Cam and Eric looked at Aunt Molly.

They laughed, too.

A Cam Jansen
Memory Game

Take another look at the picture on page 6.

Study it.

Blink your eyes and say, *"Click!"*

Then turn back to this page

and answer these questions:

1. Is anyone wearing a hat?

2. Are Cam's eyes open or closed?

3. What's written on the sign above Cam's head?

4. Is anyone wearing a blue striped shirt?

5. Does anyone have a mustache?

6. What color is Eric's jacket?